Three Ducks Went Wandering

by Ron Roy

Pictures by Paul Galdone

SCHOLASTIC INC.
New York Toronto London Auckland Sydney

For Frances Keene, a great lady and dear friend –R.R.

ISBN 0-590-30361-9

Text copyright © 1979 by Ron Roy. Illustrations copyright © 1979 by Paul Galdone. All rights reserved. This edition is published by Scholastic Inc., 730 Broadway, New York, NY 10003, through kind arrangement with The Seabury Press, Inc.

12 11 10 9 8 7 6 5 4   1 2 3/9

Printed in the U.S.A.   08

One fine day three little ducks
wandered away from their mother's nest.
They waddled past the barn and across the field,
RIGHT IN FRONT OF...

…A BIG, ANGRY BULL!
"What are those three ducks
doing in my field?"
said the bull.
"I'll teach them a lesson!"

With a snort the bull lowered his head
and charged at the ducks.

"Look," said the first little duck.

"Grasshoppers!" said the second little duck.

"Let's get them," said the third little duck.

So they scrambled under the fence

to get the grasshoppers,

and the bull crashed into the fence.

The three ducks gobbled up the grasshoppers

and then went wandering on through the woods,
RIGHT IN FRONT OF...

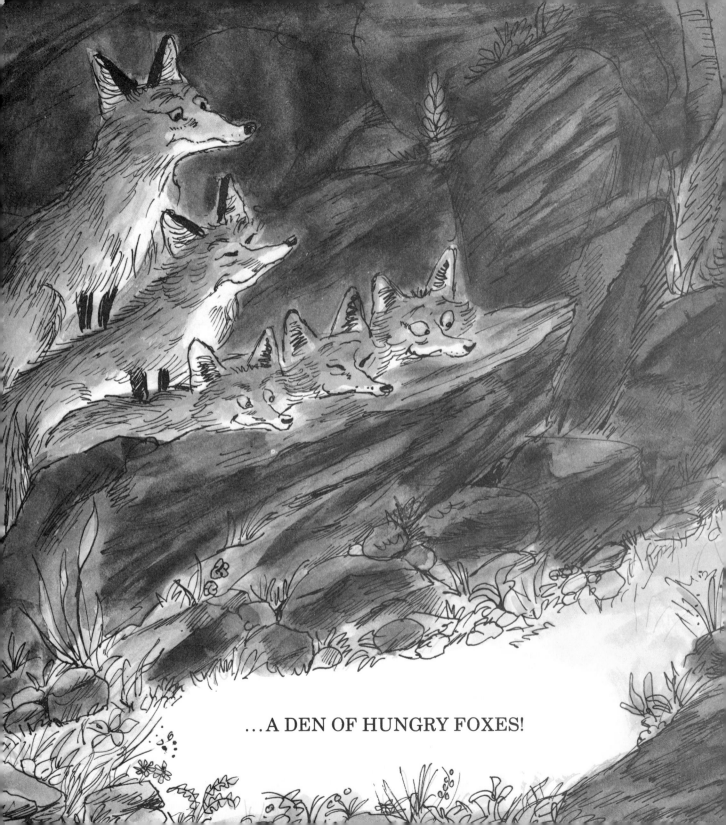

...A DEN OF HUNGRY FOXES!

"Look at those ducks walking down our path,"
said Mother Fox.
"Let's have them for our lunch," said Father Fox.
"Yes, yes!" said the little foxes.
So they all ran after the ducks.

"Look," said the first little duck.
"A pond!" said the second little duck.
"Let's go swimming," said the third little duck.

So the three of them swam out into the cool water,

and all the foxes stayed on the shore,
for they did not like to get wet.

The three ducks had a lovely long swim.
Then they paddled to the other side of the pond,
RIGHT UNDER...

...A HAWK SOARING IN THE SKY!
"Look at those fat little ducks down there,"
said the hawk.
"I'll eat one right now,
and take the other two home to my children."
With a slap of her wings, the hawk zoomed
down, down, down
toward the ducks.

"Look," said the first little duck.

"Lots of bugs!" said the second little duck.

"Let's get them," said the third little duck.

So they dived to the bottom,

and the hawk flew away hungry.

The three ducks had a yummy lunch,
and then waddled ashore to lie in the sun,
RIGHT IN FRONT OF...

…A LONG SHINY SNAKE!
"Look at those three ducks lying in the sun,"
said the snake.
"I'll eat one for lunch, and one for supper,
and one for breakfast tomorrow."

With a wiggle, the snake slithered up to the ducks.

"Look," said the first little duck.
"Butterflies!" said the second little duck.
"Let's get them," said the third little duck.

The ducks leaped into the air after the butterflies,

and the snake tied itself in knots.

By now the three ducks were very tired,
so they wandered back to the barnyard again,
RIGHT IN FRONT OF...

...THEIR MOTHER!

"Here are my three darling ducks," she said.

"You look ready for a nap."

So Mother Duck spread her wings over her children,
and the three little ducks went right to sleep.